NICK JR.

Little Bill

A Trip to the Hospital

by Kim Watson

illustrated by Mark Salisbury

Simon Spotlight/Nick Jr.

New York   London   Toronto   Sydney   Singapore

Based on the TV series *Little Bill*® created by Bill Cosby as seen on Nick Jr.®

SIMON SPOTLIGHT
An imprint of Simon & Schuster Children's Publishing Division
1230 Avenue of the Americas, New York, New York 10020
Copyright © 2001 Viacom International Inc. All rights reserved.
NICKELODEON, NICK JR., and all related titles, logos, and characters are trademarks of
Viacom International Inc. *Little Bill* is a trademark of Smiley, Inc.
All rights reserved including the right of reproduction in whole or in part in any form.
SIMON SPOTLIGHT and colophon are registered trademarks of Simon & Schuster.
Manufactured in the United States of America
First Edition
10 9 8 7 6 5 4 3 2 1
ISBN 0-689-84000-4

It was a great day to play outside.

"Giddyap! Giddyap! Yeee-ha!" Little Bill yelled. Fuchsia was right behind him.

"Yeah! I'm a cowgirl! Yeee-ha!" she said.

Little Bill lifted his ten-gallon hat and waved it in the air. "I'm a cowboy. Giddyap, giddyap, giddyap!"

Little Bill and Fuchsia laughed as they galloped around the yard.

Suddenly Little Bill tripped. "Oomph!" he said. He hit his arm on the bench and fell with a *thud!*

"Ow!" Little Bill cried.

"Are you all right?" Fuchsia asked.

Alice the Great heard Little Bill's cry and hurried out to the yard.

"What happened, Little Bill?" she asked.

"I was playing cowboy and I . . . I fell," said Little Bill. "I want Mama!"

"We'll call your Mama at work, but I think we'd better let our friend Dr. Clinkscales take a look at that arm," said Alice the Great.

Little Bill yelled, "NOOOO!"

Alice the Great whispered, "Don't worry, it's going to be all right. Now let's get you to the hospital, Little Bill. The doctor needs to look at your arm."

At the hospital, Little Bill looked up and down the hallway. "My arm still hurts," he whimpered. "I wish Mama was here. Where's Mama?"

Little Bill didn't see her anywhere.

Just then, as if by magic, Brenda came through the hospital doors.
"Little Bill!" she called.

Little Bill looked up. "Mama!" he yelled when he saw his mother. "Mama, I hurt my arm," he said.

Brenda hugged him gently. "I know, sweetie. Dr. Clinkscales will take care of that, and I'll be with you every step of the way."

"But I don't want to see him, Mama," Little Bill said.

A nurse led them down the hall.
"Look, Little Bill," said Brenda. "It's
Dr. Clinkscales, your teacher's husband."

Dr. Clinkscales smiled. "Well, hello there, Little Bill," he said. Then he took them into his office.

Little Bill looked around. "Is my teacher here?" he asked.

"I'm afraid not, but I'll be sure to tell her that I saw one of her favorite students," said Dr. Clinkscales.

That made Little Bill feel a little better.

Little Bill told the doctor what happened.

"Well, I'd better take a look at your arm," said Dr. Clinkscales as he carefully lifted Little Bill's arm. "Now, this might hurt a bit."

"You can squeeze my finger if it hurts," Brenda whispered to Little Bill.

Little Bill grabbed his mother's finger and held it tight. "Ouch!" said Little Bill as he flinched.

The doctor touched another part of Little Bill's arm. "Does it hurt here, too?" he asked. Little Bill nodded.

"Well, I'll take care of that," said Dr. Clinkscales. "You're a brave cowboy, Little Bill. You're doing great."

Dr. Clinkscales finished checking Little Bill's arm. "I feel better already," Little Bill said. "Can we go home now?"

Dr. Clinkscales laughed. "And miss getting an X-ray? It's everybody's favorite thing!"

But Little Bill was afraid. He had never gotten an X-ray before.

"Dr. Clinkscales would never do anything that wasn't good for you, honey," Brenda said tenderly.

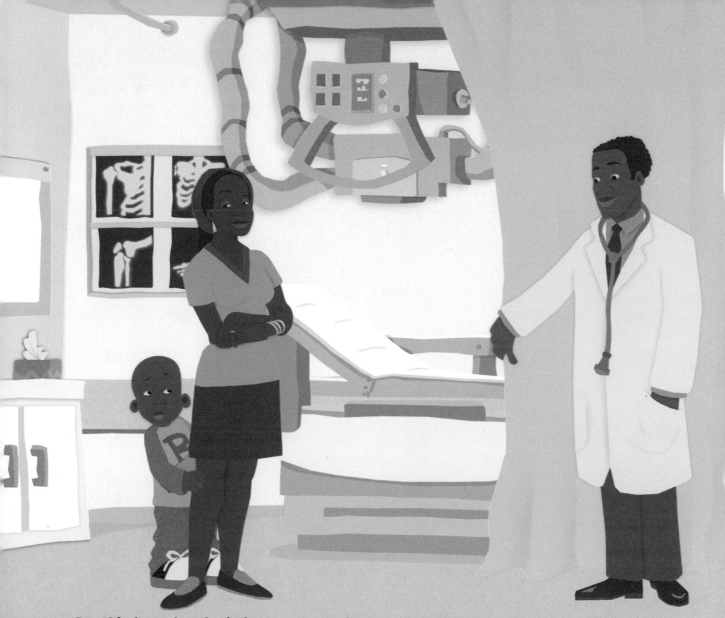

Dr. Clinkscales led them to another room. "An X-ray machine is just a great big camera," he said as he pulled back a curtain. "Only, it takes pictures of your bones, like *those*."

"They look like the dinosaur bones at the museum," said Little Bill.

Suddenly Little Bill imagined there was music everywhere. He was spinning and jumping and dancing all around the room with his dinosaur friend.

Little Bill laughed. He never knew dancing with a dinosaur could be so much fun!

And when they finally stopped dancing, and the music stopped playing, Little Bill wasn't afraid of the X-ray machine anymore!

Brenda saw the smile on Little Bill's face. "I don't think a silly old X-ray machine can frighten my little boy," she said with a wink.

"Not as long as you're here, Mama," Little Bill said.

Then he turned to the doctor and tugged on his sleeve. "I'm ready, Dr. Clinkscales."

So Dr. Clinkscales put a special X-ray apron on Little Bill. He moved the camera around on Little Bill's arm. "Now all you have to do is lie still for a minute. . . ."

A moment later Dr. Clinkscales said, "Okay, all done!"

Brenda clapped. "You did it, Little Bill. I'm proud of you!"

"And it didn't hurt!" Little Bill shouted.

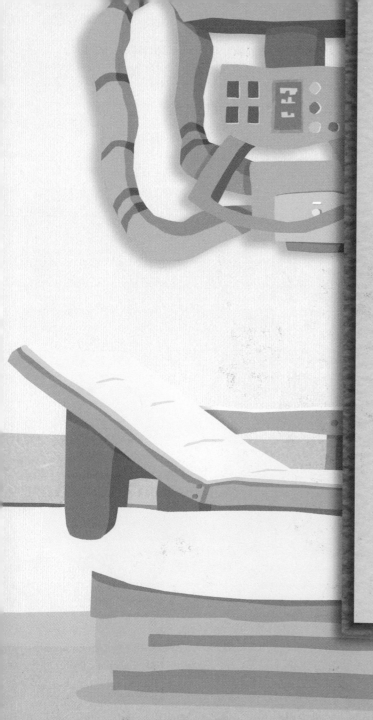

Dr. Clinkscales looked at the X-ray. "I'm afraid you've broken your arm, Little Bill," he said. "We'll have to put it in a cast."

"A cast? What's that?" Little Bill asked.

"A cast is a hard shell that keeps you from moving your arm while it heals," said Dr. Clinkscales.

"Hard like a shell on a turtle's back?"

"Exactly! And when we take it off, your arm will be as good as new," answered the doctor.

Then, for being so brave, Dr. Clinkscales gave Little Bill an X-ray of his arm. "My X-ray!" shouted Little Bill. "I can't wait to show this to my friends. Thanks!"

As they headed home, Little Bill decided he would be a doctor, just like Dr. Clinkscales.

"Yep," he said. "I'm going to be a doctor AND a cowboy. Giddyap, giddyap!"